About the Author

In the course of my forty years as a veterinary practitioner in the north east of Scotland, I have encountered a wide range of pets and owners. Some have amazed me with their tireless devotion to much loved pets; some have astounded me with their strange requests and some have frankly annoyed me with their absolute reluctance to pay their bills.

In the collection of incidents (which did happen) are the more memorable moments of my career covering a wide range of happenings – some hilarious, some serious and some very sad.

A pre-requisite for a vet is the ability to deal with different situations with tact, patience and humour. An extremely supportive and understanding wife and family, receptionists and a reliable car also go a long way to making life more bearable. Despite being called out at some ungodly hour or during a family get together, being a veterinary surgeon has been a privilege and a pleasure.

The author belongs to and lives in Aberdeen with his wife, Yvonne. Their daughter, Fiona, lives close by while their son, Colin is now resident in Northern Ireland.

A Variety of Veterinary Adventures

James Cameron Weir

Illustrated by Norman Matheson

A Variety of Veterinary Adventures

Olympia Publishers
London

www.olympiapublishers.com
OLYMPIA PAPERBACK EDITION

A CIP catalogue record for this title is
available from the British Library.

ISBN: 978-1-78830-798-7

This book is a memoir. It reflects the author's present recollections
of experiences over time. Some characteristics have been changed,
some events have been compressed, and some dialogue has been
recreated.

First Published in 2021

Olympia Publishers
Tallis House
2 Tallis Street
London
EC4Y 0AB

Printed in Great Britain

Dedication

To Andrew, Johnny, Robert and Alex

Acknowledgements

It would not have been possible to write my book without the help and assistance of those who gave so much of their time and effort in its preparation.

Yvonne, Fiona and Colin were there at all times with their support and encouragement.

Rachel and Sheila moulded the articles into an acceptable format, while Norman's illustrations gave that 'little bit' extra. Marcus, Douglas, Craig and Alistair gave valued advice.

I was fortunate to have the assistance of those of *The Leopard, Scottish Field* who published the initial articles and, Olympia, who compiled them into book form.

THE BEGINNING

After five years of a mixture of study and socialising my first day of employment started two days after graduation.

I had been offered a locum for two weeks at the Belmont Road Practice belonging to two unique vets. One was tall, bald and outgoing, while the other was quiet, thoughtful and discreet. There was a strict dress code: suit, collar, tie and clean shoes, the underlying rationale being that "shoddy clothes equal shoddy work".

There was some trepidation — but why? Following

graduation, everything should be straightforward and simple. What an illusion. Black and white areas at college were now varying shades of grey. The practice principal advised that it was the same for everyone and that you never stopped learning, but at all times to remember that you were always one step away from disaster and that you were only as good as your last case.

My first case was a ginger cat with a lump on its back. According to the textbook, it could only be a cyst, abscess or growth. In reality however, it was a hair matt as a result of a flea infection.

An urgent farm call was made to a recently-calved cow with "the staggers" (or so the farmer said on the telephone). On arrival I discovered the cow on its side with its legs and head convulsing — just as the farmer had reported. The problem had arisen from a sudden loss of magnesium in its circulation. The remedy was straightforward and simple: an injection of a magnesium solution into the blood stream, so the book said. What the book did *not* say was that it was far from easy to initially locate a vein and then infuse the magnesium solution while the cow 'staggered' about, becoming more fractious by the minute. To overcome the uncontrollable tremors, as well as reduce potential injury to both the vet and the farmer, the textbook indicated that sedation was required, but omitted to state that the consequences of such a procedure were either resolution or death. Unfortunately, the cow died. My bosses' words, "one step from disaster; as good as one's last case" immediately sprang to mind, but the resilient north-east farmer summarised matters with, "You did your best, Vet. It wasn't your fault. I thought it was going to die."

During my first weekend on call, there was a request form Hazlehead Zoo to attend a seal with gastroenteritis. This was the first weekend the zoo had opened, so it was with difficulty that my car had to push its way through the mass of Aberdeen citizens keen to inspect the new facility. The combination of 'sick seal being treated by a vet' was a real crowd-puller. The report in Monday's local paper highlighted the incident, but omitted to inform readers that, in fact, the seal had died.

And so, the first week ended, 'puppy' vet realising that there was much more to being a vet in practice than one would ever realise.

DO AS I DO

As in many walks of life, the ease of the professional to convey a sense of calm and correctness often belies the fact that mishaps are a fairly common occurrence.

Complacency may result from observing experienced practitioners getting everything right. The newly-qualified vet might think, "If they can do it — why can't I?"

The answer, of course, is experience.

As a new graduate, if you considered you knew it all, you would soon learn from watching your more mature colleagues that in fact you knew very little of the everyday realities of veterinary practice.

Things can go wrong as often as they go right. Failures occur to the anxiety of the animal's owner, not to mention the vet. Some accident-prone assistants are banned from farms when their administrations result in the death of an animal.

On one such occasion, no amount of experience could have saved the animals. Six cows were electrocuted. The hopeless vet was correct beyond doubt — the cows were dead.

Yew trees are frequently present in graveyards. While the graveyard's inhabitants are already dead, any animal eating the leaves of a yew tree will soon be dead too. All parts of a yew tree contain a highly poisonous substance which has a strong depressive effect on the heart.

Commonly there is sudden death without clinical symptoms. Imagine a young vet following an early morning call on a Sunday to find, on arrival, several cattle were dead, much to the consternation of the farmer.

As no other cattle in the field were exhibiting any clinical signs, an immediate post-mortem was required. Yew tree leaves were found in the stomach, which prompted the young vet to recall frequently-asked questions posed by external examiners in oral exams.

"Mr Smith, which plants are poisonous to animals?" This unusual question could unnerve students as this was a subject not fully covered in lectures.

The young vet, however, achieved unbridled success when a more senior vet in the practice was unable to take a blood sample from a cow. Having perfected this task at college, it was not a problem for the young vet. Being satisfied with the process, an uncompleted signed cheque was given by the farmer. The senior colleague was less than impressed.

A considerable failure occurred at a farm close to Stonehaven. When dehorning calves, the recently qualified vet inadvertently injected local anaesthetic into a vein. Due to the irritant nature of the drug, the calf reared up only to drop down stone dead. Nevertheless, the account was settled. This farmer did not believe in cheques and instead utilised a unique form of payment — cash by registered post.

Abuse of any kind to staff is now not tolerated, but one young lady vet had no intention of making a complaint. She returned to the practice and regaled her colleagues with the news that while visiting a farm owned by two unmarried brothers, she found that her bottom had been patted frequently.

In some areas in the south west of Scotland it is well known that farmers expect a very high standard from their veterinary surgeon. A female student went to observe practice where she was advised by the upmarket senior veterinary surgeon that if she were to receive a good report from college, she had to remember that there is "a right way, a wrong way and my way, so do as I do at all times." She followed the instructions to the letter even when her mentor stripped to the waist while calving a cow. It goes without saying that an excellent report was received.

Practice in the mid-fifties and sixties was a learning curve with both successes and failures, but above all, it was fun.

FROM FARRIER TO FELLOW

Although there have been veterinary surgeons in Aberdeen since 1867, William Hepburn is perhaps the only one who could be regarded as the 'father' of veterinary development in the city.

He was born in Tarland in 1875 and after leaving school at sixteen became a blacksmith's apprentice before entering Edinburgh Vet School, now the Royal (Dick) School of Veterinary Studies. He was reportedly a brilliant student qualifying in 1900 aged twenty-five. Working for a short time in Manchester and South Africa, there is an indication he served as a veterinary surgeon during the Boer War.

After returning to Scotland, he established a practice in Echt in 1901 before moving to Aberdeen and taking over the established practice of James Thompson in 1908 at Flourmill Brae, which is now a Marks and Spencers following a redevelopment of the area.

In 1910 he moved to 74 Shiprow and set up a branch at 19 Jopps Lane which is now Aberdeen Office Supplies. At that time, veterinary surgeons were also farriers, so the former blacksmith was ideally qualified to develop a niche practice for the many horses used to draw trams and for the transportation of fish, coal, milk, bread and freight from harbour shipping companies and — no doubt — also for funerals.

There was additional work for the dray horses, which were available for hire at sixpence per trip to assist with heavy loads up steep Market Street to Union Street.

The horses were guided by tracer boys who collected at Guild Street, awaiting the next load. In the mid-1940s, it was a school boy's delight to watch the four horses in action with sparks flying from their metal shoes.

From 1910 until 1934, he built a well-respected practice within the city where Hepburn was the official veterinary surgeon. In addition, he was honorary veterinary surgeon for both agricultural and urban events. Hepburn attended the Highland Show as assistant vet and was in attendance at Balmoral during the reign of both Edward VII and George V.

The establishment of a plug-in central operated system at Bon Accord Street manned by female operators during the day and by men at night, provided means of communication in both urban and rural areas.

Hepburn served during the First World War as a lieutenant in the Army Veterinary Corps but his duration of service was short. Being in a reserved occupation, he was of greater benefit to the agricultural sector than serving in the army so he returned to Aberdeen where he became a member of the local reserves.

In addition to his routine work, his thirst for academic interests resulted in the award of a fellowship from the College of Veterinary Surgeons for a thesis on anthrax — an often-fatal disease in both animals and humans.

Some fifteen years later, he achieved an additional fellowship for a clinical survey of transit fever in bovines.

Although a hard taskmaster, he never delegated a job he could not perform himself.

After operating on a savage lion from a circus visiting the town, which no other vet in Great Britain would go near, his reputation was vastly enhanced. Which anaesthetic he utilised is unknown but it was presumably something powerful enough to keep the animal sedated.

In the early 1900s, motor cars were rare in the city and although expensive, they proved useful and indispensable for further expansion of rural parts of the practice.

While trying to start Hepburn's newly acquired Daimler, the assistant was unaware of the folly of having it in gear, and as a result, the car shot forward over the assistant, and down Flourmill Brae, across St Nicholas Street, coming to rest in a shop window. Amazingly the assistant only sustained facial bruising and there were no other casualties.

The subsequent discussion between assistant and

employer would no doubt have been robust.

The practice in Shiprow was behind the Douglas Hotel in Market Street and a passage between the two still exists. Along with two colleagues, the hotel management kindly allowed us to walk past the Douglas ballroom of yesteryear and into the actual practice.

Why there was such a passage can only be imagined.

COWS, CARS AND COFFEE

An advert for an assistant in the mid-1860s indicated the applicant was to have 'good testimonials as to ability and sobriety' and be a good horseman. Salary two guineas per week and live out.' Prior to entry to veterinary college, an applicant was required to be 'able to write from dictation, parse a simple sentence as well as be acquainted with the first four rules of arithmetic, addition, subtraction, division and multiplication'. In the mid-1960s, an advert indicated 'accommodation, salary £1500 per year, free use of practice car'. Requirements for entry to veterinary college were rather simpler; three Highers, two Lowers — unlike today's requirement of four As, three Bs by the end of S5 and advanced Highers in Chemistry and Biology from S6 at a B grade minimum.

As an assistant, you are expected to allow a student to observe the daily routine; in this case, it was a female student, who, on one particular day was fortunate to be present for three cases.

The first required assistance at Porthlethen for a sow farrowing. As the sow was recumbent, any assistance required a horizontal vet amidst straw, manure and an enhancing aroma. The number of piglets increased to twelve, delighting the farmer and amazing the student.

Prior to leaving the farm, the routine was to use the farm phone to contact the receptionist/typist/nurse/dog groomer at the surgery, who passed on any additional calls. The next case was a prolapsed womb at a dairy farm in Udny, which required immediate help.

At that time, the practice car was a two-litre GT Ford Cortina, capable of considerable velocity. On the Cannahars Straight, towards Udny, our speed was greatly in excess of the legal limit.

On arrival at the farm, the student was rather pale and almost fainted when she saw the magnitude of the everted womb. The action of drugs to contract the womb and to lessen the ability of the cow to strain, enabled the vet, with a degree of manual dexterity, muscular endeavour and sweat, to reverse the prolapse. Frequently, a dram was suggested; however, in general it was safer to stick to coffee — although the student was totally unnerved when she was left with a cup handle when the cup itself crashed to the floor.

The final call was to a small holding in Skene, where a sheep was unable to lamb. The road via Dyce and

Kingswells had several sharp bends, but the reinforced disc brake pads enabled speed to be maintained with precision, although this may not have been the student's viewpoint. She had never been so scared in her life.

Examination indicated twins but as the sheep had a narrow pelvis, a Caesarean section was required. Half an hour later, two live lambs were 'extracted' and, as nature intended, they immediately started to suckle (amazing the student even more).

On returning to Holland, the student wrote to express her appreciation of her time in Aberdeen, but remarked that the assistant was a "more a racing driver than a vet".

THE MAGIC OF MARTS

A recent series on BBC 1 highlighted the many varied aspects of Aberdeen and Northern Marts.

Prior to the development of auction marts, fairs and local markets were the setting for the buying and selling of livestock.

Later sales were conducted on farms by independent auctioneers who advertised their services in local newspapers.

Auction sales were introduced in 1868 with regular marts in twenty county towns in Aberdeenshire, principally Turriff, Maud, Inverurie and Ellon where two independent firms operated on opposite sides of the same street.

Within Aberdeen, Kittybrewster became the

agricultural hub for both city and shire with several independently owned firms which were institutions in themselves.

The Central Mart, opened in 1883, introduced a new concept of ownership with the firm being both owned and controlled by its farmer shareholders. In 1898 the enterprising directors let for a "consideration" of £65, a field to Aberdeen Football Club for a season.

The presence of a railway station at Kittybrewster greatly assisted in the movement of cattle from country areas. While this was the initial death knell of local markets, it assisted in the development of southern markets especially London. Between 1850 and 1870, forty thousand cattle were transported south. One adverse effect of such transportation was that the cattle reached their destination in a "tired and fevered" state so that the meat following slaughter was not of top quality. This difficulty was overcome by slaughtering prior to transporting; the condition of the meat then reaching the southern markets being "far superior" to that of cattle exported live.

During the 1940s, a series of takeovers and amalgamations accentuated the closure of the local county marts leading, in 1947, to the founding of Aberdeen and Northern Marts.

By the 1950s the firm was able to make available to sellers their payment on the day of sale. A guarantee which still stands today. Many farmers work by themselves, often in social isolation so the weekly mart enables personal contacts to be made, as well as allowing agricultural transactions to be completed with local representatives of a diverse range of firms — mechanical, seed, feed and clothing.

Banking facilities are also at hand as well as an enterprising veterinary surgeon. Mart work formed a large part of the practice with early morning calls from the numerous cattle dealers who wanted to ensure that their stock had no ailments prior to entering the auction ring. Cattle dealers were unique in many ways, having both the trained eye and the financial where-with-all to purchase "good quality animals".

Their expensive clothing was a reflection of the "upmarket" areas in which they resided. Quite what their neighbours thought of their smelly, manure-stained vehicles is a mystery. Mart work was often of an urgent nature — frequently being requested at the most awkward times — middle of the night, attending church or worst of all just as you were sitting down to tea with the family. Our caretaker at the time was a very positive person, to whom nothing was a problem; this extended to "calving a cow". The surgery receiving such a request about six p.m. (evening surgery at seven p.m.). He, without hesitation rushed to the mart to calve the cow with a degree of efficiency which would put any vet to shame in a mode of dress totally devoid of hygiene — cord trousers with red braces and incredibly, his baffies (slippers). He was a firm favourite with the mart staff who derived much pleasure in reminding future young vets faced with a similar task that the caretaker could do the job more quickly than you and "he never sent a bill".

Like their predecessors the mart directors are astute individuals — one example being the development in 1989 of electronic sales whereby stock could be sold by computer to buyers throughout Britain.

Mart workers, always smartly dressed, were under the close eye of a supervisor — who controlled everyone with military precision — even the vets. Drovers (workers who managed the movement of stock) were enthusiastic in their approach. One can recall during the 1940s, prior to the motorised movement of stock, the drovers were responsible for the transfer of stock from the outskirts of the city to the mart through residential areas, where small boys (such as myself and my brother) were delighted when an animal escaped from the herd to decimate one of the well-kept gardens — much to the annoyance of the householder.

After some forty-three years the marts relocated from Kittybrewster to a new, four million pound purpose built centre at Thainstone near Inverurie. The combination of established basic principles assisted by modern means of communication, technology and animal welfare is reflected in an annual throughput of livestock in the region of ninety-five thousand animals valued at about £90million.

The inclusion of dining facilities allows increasing numbers of retired farmers, agricultural workers and the general public to mix with those of today's generation with the ongoing discussion — *'well in my day'.* While the local "lingo" with its own Doric foundation is unique, the success of the organisation is the in-built trust between employer, employee, buyer, seller, valuer and auctioneer, which enables one-to-one decisions to be reached on a fair and equable basis.

Personal conversation will always be far superior to "computer talk", email or answering machines that don't reply, thereby ensuring the future of Aberdeen and Northern Marts.

A PINK ELEPHANT ON

PARADE

A vet, unknown outside Yorkshire, discovered while watching a TV sports report that the Birmingham City goalkeeper was called James Herriot. He decided that this would be a suitable pen name as, at that time, the Veterinary Ethics Committee had indicated that if a book was published under his own name this would be regarded as "advertising". In his writing career he published fourteen veterinary books and eight books for children. Two films were produced from the books as well as a television series.

By a unique coincidence the first film *All Creatures Great and Small*, was to be screened at the Regal Cinema (now Vue, Shiprow) at the same time as the annual Aberdeen Festival Parade. With some difficulty, the secretary of the local branch of the British Veterinary Association persuaded his colleagues that the film could be "advertised" by the inclusion of a float in the Festival Parade.

As is often the case, several of those who were in favour of the enterprise, were found to have "urgent cases" to attend to on the Saturday of the parade. As a consequence, only three vets, their wives and children arrived at Rossleigh Commercial Garage (now the Land Rover Centre) where the enthusiastic manager provided a forty foot articulated vehicle. Such was his zeal for the project that he insisted on supplying an electrician, a painter, a signwriter and a driver to help.

Progress was on schedule until, to our horror, we realised certain key items were missing. Watt and Grant, a department store no longer in existence, had kindly offered to donate some oversized model animals used to attract children to their toy department. As time was short these had to be collected immediately. Thus the driver was quickly dispatched to pick them up. A quiet and composed man, he was flabbergasted to learn that he had to collect a lion, a horse, two giraffes and... a pink elephant.

The animals were lined up on the pavement outside the shop awaiting collection. The pink elephant, in particular attracted the attention of many children who came to talk to it, resulting in even more delay. In his haste, the frustrated driver forgot to secure the rear van door which swung open and hit a lamppost. No animal was injured, therefore no vet required.

These animals joined a large mounted fish and three live sheep from the zoo. Fencing was provided by the nursery, William Smith at Hazlehead, while the BBC in Beechgrove Terrace provided a sound system accompanied by a tape of "animal noises".

The cinema had agreed to provide film posters to display on the float. However, when the signwriter began to merge the posters and his placards of the sponsors of the float, he discovered that instead of *All Creatures Great and Small*, they had sent posters of Richard Todd in *Angels 15*. The manager of the cinema was none too pleased.

Finally, as the completed float was about to leave the garage, one of the vet's wives noticed the misspelling of the word veterinary. After a few moments of panic, the signwriter swiftly resolved the problem.

The parade from Carden Place down Union Street to the Beach Boulevard was well attended and attracted much attention, especially the float from which could be heard a roaring lion and a trumpeting pink elephant. The vets and accompanying families thoroughly enjoyed the trip and were ecstatic to be awarded the silver cup for the best float.

On that evening a specially invited audience enjoyed a private viewing of *All Creatures Great and Small*. The film proved to be so popular it was screened for six weeks.

So, the advertising was successful.

IN THE FAST LANE

Vacancies advertised in the *Veterinary Record* in the 1960s routinely indicated "assistant required, accommodation and car provided, interview expenses paid". The only really important feature was "the car".

This, however could be misleading. Depending on the view of the senior partner, "car" could mean a van, a battered dirty second hand vehicle used by the previous assistant, or a new car. I was fortunate — a green Triumph Herald with no caveat regarding practice use only. FRG 964 D was unique in that to fill up with oil and water, two clips at the edge of the front body panel had to be released so that the entire section could then be tipped forward. It was also memorable in that it was our honeymoon car.

Senior partners were of course to be considered as

veterinary surgeons and not just vets, some adopting a God-like persona. The difference between such a veterinary surgeon and God was that God realized he was not a veterinary surgeon. Their automobiles reflected their status, ranging from a Bristol, Lotus, Mercedes Benz and for one unique individual, a Rolls Royce. Others were more modest with an Austin, Morris or Ford. One such car — a Ford Prefect — after its veterinary life was over became a nun's car. I can but trust that the language befitted its new owner.

Even with a car, punctuality was a personal failing. While a delayed arrival may be acceptable, reading the time of a wedding as three p.m. as opposed to two p.m. was almost unforgivable. The bridal car was making its way to the reception as we made our way to the church.

Over the years as a family we have experienced some thirty-two motor cars: some good, some very good, some bad, one very bad and some with tales to relate. The worst by far was an Austin Marina. It was unstable, would not corner with any precision and worst of all, could not exceed 60 mph. The number plate starting with HUF was horribly accurate — hopeless, useless, functionless. It had to go. One unforgettable day, cars were required for myself, assistant and my wife — so I purchased three Triumph Vitesses. The salesman was ecstatic, the bank manager less so.

The best road car was one I had longed for — a BMW 728. It could out corner, and out accelerate any other car with 100 mph well within its capability. It had one major failing, it was useless in fields so had to be replaced, much to the amusement of local vets who, quite unjustly, referred to it as Boastful Mad Weir's car. A succession of Volvos followed with which there were many adventures. The first one had the unique registration of JAG 190V which was transferred to each successive Volvo. One enterprising vet had the registration VET 1 but following a complaint, the Royal College of Veterinary Surgeons decreed that as it was a form of advertising such a number plate was therefore not allowable.

Some fifty years on similar registrations are relatively common but they should be avoided on up-market cars as this creates the impression that the practice fees are too high. Although the Volvos were mechanically sound, on one occasion the gear box jammed in reverse some six miles from the Volvo garage. Despite being ill advised, possibly illegal, the journey was accomplished in reverse gear.

During the winter months when snow was much more frequent and severe than it is now, studded winter tyres ensured mobility. There was one potential problem. Due to their greater weight it was imperative to ensure that the wheel nuts were tight enough to avoid them becoming slack. The senior partner, no less, observed the rear wheel passing the front of his car, ending the journey prematurely. (Such tyres were later banned.) Before trading in a vet's car, it was advisable to at least wash it, but despite thorough cleaning, the routine in all garages was to send it to auction as it was not possible to eliminate the lingering smells. One business-orientated practice principal, aware of the poor trade-in value of such cars, overcame this difficulty by negotiating with a young car salesman, agreeing a trade-in valuation on his wife's car, and then substituting an assistant's well-used car, for the new car. The car salesman was not impressed.

Overall, the best car was a Ford two litre Cortina GT. It was unique in many ways — there were only two in town, a fish merchant owning the other. They were an eye-catching yellow with every bit of chrome the manufacture could add. As it was a new model, or possibly a Friday night car, it was prone to problems. It might not start, the steering lock would not unlock, brake pads wore out very quickly as did the clutch. These difficulties were not for the driver to attend to but the responsibility of the service manager who was reputed to become very anxious when told, "The vet is on the phone."

One evening just prior to evening surgery, the car appeared to run out of petrol outside a local police station. The service manager arrived very promptly to discover that the fuel line had ruptured. He suggested that if we used his car to take him home, I could have his car until mine was repaired. On arrival he suggested coming in for a cup of tea, but when his wife learned that I had not eaten said, "Well, you'll just have my husband's haddock and chips as you are short of time."

He longingly looked on as I ate his tea — now that is a good service manager.

THE ETERNAL CAT

In the 1960s, evening consultations started at seven p.m., lasting until the final client departed.

One Tuesday evening, a client clutching a Siamese cat came into the consulting room. It transpired that the cat had been bequeathed to him by his aunt. The final request from his aunt was that she wished the cat's teeth to be cleaned. As the cat's teeth were relatively clean, a more experienced vet would probably have said this was unnecessary. For a young vet, however, this was an order that had to be obeyed, and so an appointment was arranged.

On the following Wednesday, I had been joined by a student, who was 'seeing practice'. With his assistance, the cat was anaesthetised without difficulty; however, during the operation, the cat developed a heart spasm, accompanied by breathing difficulties. With the student guiding the 'master', the cat was resuscitated, thus enabling the operation to be completed, the cat's teeth by then sparkling clean.

Had I known what was in store, it might have been advantageous to flee the scene, but I had to support the client through days one, two and three, as the cat failed to recover from the anaesthetic. The cat finally passed over on the Saturday, to join its previous owner in eternity.

The student was far from impressed, muttering that the vet was incompetent and should be "struck off". The client, however, was impressed, expressing appreciation for the care and attention given to his aunt's cat. He was only too willing to settle his account, prior to departing to bury the cat in his garden. While preparing the cat's grave, on Sunday he decided he would prefer to have the cat preserved. He approached the museum in the art gallery, where the attendant indicated that the proposal was 'mad' — as was our client (a view shared by the student). As a consequence, the client contacted me on Monday.

The situation dictated that it would be useful to remember the principle 'the impossible we can do at once; miracles take a little longer'.

Universities are generally helpful in assisting with genuine enquiries. The request was directed to the Zoology Department, where a technician was only too delighted to accept the task. He indicated that six months would be required, requesting a fee of £50 (around £1000 today). The client was delighted, remarking that it would be money well spent. Six months almost to the day, the technician called to inform me he had carefully mounted the cat in a smart glass cabinet and that it was ready for collection.

The impossible had not been achieved at once, but three miracles were: the student realised that the academic aspect of learning had to be matched by the art and craft of reality, which enabled him in time to have a successful practice; the young vet, now somewhat older, had articles published in a respected magazine, and the client had a cat (unfortunately dead) which would have delighted his aunt with its sparkling clean teeth.

TONGUES APART

Fit like? Foo are ye deing? (How are you — are you well?) is a frequent greeting in the north east. This was a complete mystery to foreign incomers in the mid-1970s, whether they came from Holland, America, France or other parts of the globe. They were not tourists, but oil related workers, families and pets. It was almost possible to recognise their various countries of origin by their demeanour and dress. The Dutch were polite and smartly dressed without ostentation while Americans tended to be over positive. Uniform attire of tee-shirt, jeans and white trainers, with sun glasses perched on their head which had not been seen in Aberdeen — given the climate, this was unnecessary.

They all had their unique terms and approach. A large

overweight American man confused a receptionist by requesting an appointment "for his dog to be shot". It was only after discussion that she discovered the appointment was to have his dog vaccinated.

Further confusion arose one day as my wife was standing in for the receptionist when a young blonde American lady requested a trim for her cockapoo (cocker spaniel/poodle). Her accent was translated as a cockatoo.

Reserved Aberdonians also had their quaint terminology, frequently when a sensitive problem required attention. A genteel elderly lady leaned over the consulting table and whispered in the vet's ear that her dog had a "cold in its teapot" which proved to be her term for a penile discharge.

On the large animal side some terms took time to get to grips with. "To clean a coo" was a request to remove the foetal membranes from a cow after calving. One inexperienced receptionist retorted to the surprise of the farmer "Why can't you wash your own cow?"

A "blown coo" was a cow with its large stomach distended with gas. The remedy was simple: insert a trocar (a modified sharp knife) through the skin into the stomach. The expelled gas (methane) was instantly released but, if ignited, took the farmer by complete surprise. Some care had to be exercised to avoid setting the byre on fire, as happened to a colleague down south.

A "choked beast" was one where a mass (often a turnip) had become lodged in the gullet of a beef stirk. These cases caused anxiety to both farmer and vet. Without skill and experience in the use of a choke rope (firm long tube encased in leather) which had to be passed into the gullet, over-zealous pressure could rupture the gullet. With controlled but firm pressure, the mass could be pushed into the stomach to the relief of the beast and farmer and, more so, the vet.

Each part of the country has its own unique dialect but for each and every vet learning the local language can be more difficult than passing exams.

A body is aye learnin'!

THE KINDNESS OF CLIENTS

The bottle of premium malt whisky was accompanied by the card *"Something special for someone special"* — a gift from a gracious lady in Blairs. The much- loved family cat, after intensive treatment, had sadly been consigned to the eternal Cat Sanctuary to play for evermore.

Another kindly former client, as we shall see, was a lady whose old English sheepdog required much treatment for an extensive blood blister on its ear following a scrap with a neighbour's cat. This lady's husband had been the manager of the Royal Darroch Hotel in Cults at the time of the tragic gas explosion. A new building, the Deeside Care Home, now occupies the site.

In those days, there was a tacit understanding among vets that no vet should pay for accommodation if there was a vet nearby who could supply 'free lodgings'. Thus we had arranged to stay with a colleague of mine at Melrose, so that our families could attend the Melrose Seven-a-side Rugby Tournament. The other family was somewhat unique, having three children born in the same year. As a result, any childhood ailment affected them all. With perfect timing, our planned visit coincided with an outbreak of gastroenteritis within our host's family. On arrival with weekend gifts we were greeted with the news that on medical advice, it would be unwise for our children to stay for the weekend.

Back then, with no ATMs, this created an unexpected difficulty as not every hotel or boarding house would accept cheques and none would accept business cheques. Desperate diseases required desperate treatment, so we approached the largest hotel in the area. On arrival, the lady on the reception desk was only too willing to insist that we should stay and that a business cheque would indeed be accepted, as here was the vet who had successfully treated her dog's ear when her husband was manager of the Royal Darroch Hotel.

At the tournament, our team, the Grammar FPs, failed to qualify, so it was back to the hotel for our evening meal. After getting 'poshed up', we found our entry to the dining room was blocked by a member of the local police force bearing the amazing news that a man had entered the kitchen and stabbed the chef, so meals could not be served.

Not quite the weekend we had envisaged perhaps. The kindness of clients, however, made up for any minor inconveniences.

ZERO TO HERO

While a veterinary practice may appear to have many clients — some come and go, and some go on forever — the only client you can be absolutely sure of is the one you are attending that day. Some will be satisfied with your assistance, while others will not, you'll be in no doubt from the response. However, the majority are loyal and will forgive the occasional error.

On one occasion a client was very angry beyond belief. A colleague from Longside asked if I would be willing to examine a horse on behalf of one of his clients, prior to purchase. My colleague was unique in that he was the only vet in Great Britain who used a Bristol car as his only mode of transport. He was of the opinion that, apart from himself, I was the only vet in the area who could be depended on "to do the job correctly". As his middle name was that of my surname, I could not refuse.

During the examination, I detected that in addition to being lame, the horse was also blind, and thus advised the client that it would be unwise to purchase it. The client had promised his daughter he would buy the horse for her birthday, but now would have to break the devastating news to her. Moreover, because of this "useless vet" he would now have to find a "decent vet". I never learned the eventual outcome, but he did pay his bill. Following his retiral the Longside vet moved to Ireland, where he became a consultant to racing stables.

On another occasion, client satisfaction did occur, although a visit to a farm at Kingswells to neuter two ponies was associated with near disaster, if not mayhem. The difficulty was simple; the ponies had never been handled, so when the first pony dragged the farmer out of the stable, as opposed to the farmer leading the pony out, my assistant and I sensed potential problems. Provided a pony has been anesthetised, the surgical procedure was straightforward. However, when the needle touched the pony's neck it reared up and crashed down on my new car (luckily, it being a Volvo, neither paint nor bodywork was damaged). My assistant came to the rescue, calming down the pony and enabling the anaesthetic to be administered and the task was completed.

The second pony was even more difficult to handle so, to avoid potential difficulties in the confined space of the stable yard, I decided to take the animal across the Kingswells Road to an adjacent field. This was a major error on my part, as every time I tried to inject it, the sudden movement and noise of a car on the road made the anxious pony — not to mention the vet — even more unsettled. The solution was simple: send my assistant to stop the traffic. He was there not only to gain experience, but also to do as he was asked. All might have been well, had it not been for a low flying, very noisy helicopter, but we persevered and thereafter, all was quite simple.

Over a refreshing cup of tea, the farmer made our day by telling us that he had been dreading the job.

"But it was OK, as you boys made it so easy." I often wondered if this was the comment which prompted my assistant to move to Newmarket to become an equine veterinary surgeon. Sometime later, I bought a horse for my daughter. It was checked over by a colleague and found to be suitable. What I then discovered was that she was allergic to the horse, developing a skin reaction so severe that she required medical attention. The hard hat she was so proud of had to be discarded.

Unlike my two colleagues, I decided that small animals were less stressful. I survived twenty-five years.

IT TAKES ALL SORTS

In general practice, a variety of clients is encountered. Some are difficult and demanding, some are cheerful and charming. Others are downright terrifying.

All clients, however, expect a smart, clean surgery, this being the responsibility of the cleaner or caretaker (or today perhaps a junior nurse or one of the ardent, young animal-loving aspiring vets who are in never-ending supply). In the mid-1960s, a reliable cleaner or caretaker was difficult to find but, in our case, offering a rent-free flat above the surgery was a huge incentive.

A council employee (later discovered to be a bin man) was selected. He proved to be very diligent and efficient. Moreover, he indicated early on in his employment that 'If you want anything, I can get it for you', suggesting his willingness to oblige.

Some months later, we received the surgery gas bill. It was astronomical and far in excess of the usual amount. It turned out that his ability 'to get anything' resulted in the gas meter to the upstairs flat being connected to that of the surgery. This necessitated a new employee.

It's common practice to employ homers in the north east of Scotland. These are skilled tradesmen who undertake extra work without the knowledge of their employer or the tax man, with payment to be made in kind or preferably cash.

The ladies of the household were of the opinion that our lounge needed to be re-papered and a potential solution came to mind. A client had mentioned he was a painter and would be interested in a homer.

The cost was acceptable so he arranged to come in during his holidays, by which time the ladies had purchased wallpaper at a cost far in excess of my expectation. "You won't know the room when I'm finished!" he said.

This was indeed the case. Unfortunately, he didn't match up the wallpaper pattern and had cut many of the sheets short so that they didn't reach the skirting board. He even added another piece to try and fix the problem.

When I pointed this out, he said, "Just move the furniture in front of it."

Over a cup of tea, I asked if he'd been a painter for long. The reply was unforgettable, "Thirty years painting corporation buses."

Similarly, appointments in the affluent parts of the city always had to be treated with caution and occasional anxiety. I was called out by a family who had recently moved to Aberdeen from Edinburgh, where they were informed their dog was expecting four pups and, due to her narrow pelvis, she would require a caesarean section (in the end, six pups were born without a C-section).

The lady's husband exuded class and professionalism; his immaculate suit must have cost a fortune. He suggested a drink was in order and while he quaffed two glasses of red wine with considerable rapidity and relish, I sipped an apple juice.

During the subsequent conversation, I was never so glad to have declined an alcoholic beverage when his wife informed me that the family had come to Aberdeen following her husband's appointment as sheriff principal.

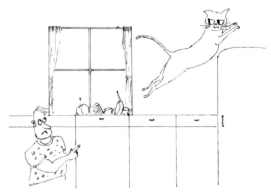

IT SHOULDN'T HAPPEN TO

A CAT

I was awakened at three a.m. by the persistent ringing of the telephone. The call was from an owner in Torry who requested a visit, as his cat's ears were shaking! Whether or not the call was genuine was difficult to determine, so I advised the caller to allow the cat to settle down for an hour and then call back if he was concerned.

At exactly four a.m. he phoned again to report that the cat was no better, repeating his request for a visit. So, there was nothing for it but to go. On my way to the address, one positive thought, at least there were fresh butteries – morning rolls - to purchase at Aitken's bakery, a busy place at that horrendous time of day.

As always with such visits, it was the top flat, to which there was a narrow stairwell with thirty-nine, almost vertical, concrete steps. By the time I reached the address, I was out of breath, as well as reflecting on the sanity of a veterinary vocation.

The door was opened by a pale faced young man,

dressed in the almost universal crushed T-shirt, dark jeans, and trainers, which at some time previously had been white. He was rather unsteady on his feet, but explained that he had a few friends in for a drink. He led me to the kitchen to see the cat. The room was untidy, with unwashed pans in an unclean sink and the floor requiring a scrub.

The black cat (no name given) on the kitchen shelf did require a visit, as by that time not only were its ears shaking — so was its head! Nevertheless, its mobility was amazing. As soon as it saw me, it was off like a missile from the kitchen shelf, via the sink, to the top of the deep freeze, where it lodged itself a few inches from the ceiling in such a way that no-one could reach it.

As there was no possibility of examining the cat, I was able to observe that despite the alarming symptoms, the cat was relatively normal. I suggested that it should be left alone and if the owner was anxious, he could call me again.

On the way out, I passed his friends, who were huddled round the fire, smoking. The sweet smell allowed an instant diagnosis — cannabis. Thereafter, the feline was referred to as the cannabis cat.

The owner did call the following morning to report that the cat was back to normal. He was appreciative of my assistance and asked me to send him the bill. This was always a suggestion to be wary of as I was unlikely to be paid — and so it transpired.

One consolation from the visit was, of course, the Aitkens buttery. As I tucked into mine, I pondered: do cats have hangovers? In all my years as a practising vet, I never did see another 'stoned cat' — but I often returned to Torry for more butteries.

AN AVIAN ADVENTURE

My veterinary series anecdotes relate to actual events which occurred during the 1960s and 1970s, when the vocational approach was more important than today where the majority of practices are business orientated with some even operating as a company. It is a moot point whether the personal trust between practitioner and client have been somewhat lost as a result.

During the time I was in practice, it was routine, as it was also in medical practices, for wives to answer telephone calls at the weekends — generally unpaid. Contact could be maintained by use of "bleepers", but it was predictable that a bleep would summon you at the most inappropriate time — whether you were in the swimming pool, pub or church. On an occasion, one such bleep sounded during a church service, rousing the sleepy. A bit of a bonus in some ways — I missed the collection! Returning home, I learned that the call was to Westhill, where an African Grey parrot had escaped while the owner was cleaning its cage.

The request was simple, "Come and rescue my parrot from a tall tree in my garden."

My nine-year-old son asked if he could come, so off we set. He became a banker not a vet.

On arrival the owner was somewhat upset as he was unable to encourage his expensive pet to leave its new perch in a sycamore tree. Although he suggested the use of an extending ladder, I declined as I have no head for heights. Often, a radical remedy is required so I enlisted the help of the fire brigade. As such a request for assistance was unique and possibly not in the operational manual, a fire officer's car accompanied by two fire engines was dispatched. The combined use of blue lights and sirens was an occurrence hitherto not experienced on the Westhill road at that time. The convoy arrived quickly, with a degree of precision which would be difficult to match, a twenty-ton vehicle requiring an experienced driver. Very quickly a large number of spectators consisting of boys on bicycles, girls with prams, dogs on leads, and adults also arrived, the latter being regarded within the emergency services as 'rubber neckers'. Such onlookers wished to observe everything, make profound and amusing suggestions as to how to resolve the crisis, becoming in their minds the control centre of the entire incident.

The officer in charge assessed the situation and instructed the crews to use a large extending ladder, and a fireman ascended it. As he reached the parrot, it flew just out of his reach, much to the amusement of the onlookers but not to his colleagues or the anxious owner. Several of the firemen endeavoured to catch the parrot but every time one of them was within touching distance the parrot flew away to perch even higher up.

"Told you so," was the supercilious comment from a know-all onlooker.

"They don't have a clue how to catch a parrot."

After about an hour, the officer in charge accepted defeat and withdrew his crew, leaving the scene rather more quietly than they had arrived, with the onlookers' glances not assisting his mood. Possibly during the return to base he came to the conclusion that his promotion prospects would be enhanced if he could prepare a manual on how to catch a parrot.

Once the firemen and spectators had departed, I suggested a simple remedy — place a generous amount of food on the floor of the cage attaching a string to close the door once the parrot was inside. After about half an hour the ploy was successful. Being a Sunday, the fee could have been doubled but it wasn't — a vocation as opposed to business.

THE HOLIDAY VET

A request from a veterinary surgeon in the Western Isles to act as a locum for two weeks sounded interesting. The trip to the Isles required a journey by car and ferry. Not knowing the vet, I requested details of how to identify him.

The response was simple, "I will be the only person on the pier wearing a jacket," — thus it transpired.

No detailed instructions were given apart from the staff: 'The staff (mature woman and aged handyman) will look after you... Never refuse the offer of a cup of tea... Here are the van keys (I was expecting a car)... Sunday is a day of rest (no papers, no petrol, park swings padlocked).'

His final advice before leaving on his Norton motorbike with backpack and fishing rod, was, "You'll be OK, no-one will ever question your diagnosis. In these parts the vet is regarded as a sort of demi-god."

I felt very lonely, as well as anxious as to what lay ahead. However, there was not much time to dwell on such matters. It was more important to discover how the cooker, dishwasher and washing machine worked, with the added hazard of making up one's bed in a room cluttered with fishing tackle and shotguns, either complete or in bits!

At college, the symptoms of every disease were black and white, but in the Western Isles every colour of the rainbow was to be expected. Every surname was prefixed by Mac and, as many of the families were interrelated, if you offended one, you offended the lot. Directions, however, were simple, as well as accurate: 'the house with the freshly painted blue door, three houses along from the Ford car on the left-hand side of the road'.

Although out-of-hours visits were infrequent (the vet having his clients well-trained), a call came in one evening from a crofter at what was possibly the furthest point from the surgery, requesting assistance for a cow 'stuck calving'. Such a call could not be refused. Speed limits were non-existent and it was amazing the speed the van could achieve. Upon arrival at the croft, the 'pied piper' syndrome was evident: the crofter, followed by his parents, his wife and several children, streamed out. They were not in the least bit interested in the cow, but only to see the new vet.

In Aberdeenshire such cases were attended to in the byre or cattle shed. To my horror, the crofter informed me that the cow was up the hill! However, transport was provided by a quad bike and after a hair-raising journey, we reached the animal. Twenty minutes later, a live female calf was delivered — more valuable than a male calf, it having greater market value. If not sold, it could be used for breeding. The delighted crofter decreed that a 'small' dram was called for. (What was a large one like?) The return journey was slower and more careful.

Alcohol and religion appear to play almost equal parts in island life, with the many pubs being outnumbered by churches. Livestock auction sales were held every Wednesday. The auction could not start without the presence of the vet, as the ministry of agriculture required pre- and post-sale health inspections. The health standard of the animals was high so this was not an onerous task. It was, in fact, enjoyable. The ringside conversation, aided and abetted by the repartee from the auctioneer, would have given the review group *Scotland The What?* a field day.

Towards the end of the two weeks, a visit to the north end of the island revealed an interesting facet of the Western Isles' life. After attending to a sheep, I was invited by the middle-aged lady into the house for tea and freshly-baked, buttered scones. It was, with amazement, that I learned that with the underlying church influence in such areas, there was an enduring commitment to family life.

Following education, the girls of the household frequently attended university in mainland Scotland.

After graduation, many of them remained, gaining full-time employment, marrying and not returning to their native islands.

As a consequence, many of their male classmates remained, but their marriage prospects were much reduced, not helped by the complication of attending to ageing parents within the family home.

Many did not marry until their parents passed away, or if they did marry, their wives appreciated the family priorities — the elderly parents came first, her husband, second, the dog, third and herself, last. She was such a wife.

Thus ended a trip into another world with no social pretentions and a community that was willing to accept a 'holiday vet' into their society. Indeed, it was a case of, 'happy to meet, sorry to part, happy to meet again'.

EVERLASTING LOVE

When the issues fail beyond recovery, humanitarian consideration must at all times take precedence over any emotional aspect, however difficult it may be. Tending to the pet is the veterinary surgeon's first responsibility but care and consideration has also to be given to the owners, this being exceptionally difficult if the parents elect to be accompanied by their children. Several parents consider that enjoyment and sorrow are part of having a pet with loss and bereavement part and parcel of family life.

I can recall a young couple who had recently arrived

in the city with an aged dog which unexpectedly had passed away. Their attachment to their pet was such that they intended to return to Kent at the weekend, five days hence, to bury their pet in the family garden. The request from them was very simple, can you help us "preserve" the dog for the journey. Not so simple. As a student I had worked during a summer vacation in a fish house and seen first-hand that ice could be utilised to preserve fish for the train journey to the London markets. Would the same therefore not be possible for the dog? One of the benefits of belonging to the Granite City is that with the assistance of old school friends the impossible can become possible. The outcome of a phone call to a friend in the fish trade resulted in some ice being set aside for collection, no charge as we both went to the grammar school. What I had not expected was that "some" ice was *one ton.* Nevertheless, the young couple was delighted, packing a vast quantity of ice around their pet, recumbent in the car boot. I never heard from them again but I often speculated on the eventual outcome of a long journey with melting ice.

Another client had a similar problem, wishing to inter his pet in Wales. For him the problem was simply solved by persuading his boss to assist. He was successful, being allowed the use the company helicopter for the journey.

A new receptionist was quite at a loss when she received a telephone call from a firm of solicitors requesting assistance in fulfilling the instructions in a client's will. She handed over the telephone with a look inferring that this place is crazy. The instructions were specific and straightforward — contact Mr Weir, arrange with Galloway and Sykes, a cabinet maker of some repute, to make a silk lined coffin and the gardener to prepare a plot in the garden. When all arrangements were in hand, the gardener, housekeeper, family solicitor, doctor and vet would attend the interment at which Mr Weir, as her church elder, would know what to say. Thereafter tea would be served in the house along with some of her favourite Harvey's Bristol Cream sherry. The inscribed granite headstone is still visible in the garden of the family home in Bieldside.

For those unable to utilise their garden either as it was non-existent, was too small or too close to difficult neighbours, the availability of a pet cemetery just outside the city boundary filled the void. There an individual plot was available to which could be added a tree or a headstone. These who had lost a much-loved pet had a permanent place of solace and comfort which they could visit as frequently as they wished for as long as they wished. In the early seventies a pet owner, following the departure of his pet discovered that the nearest pet crematorium was in the south of England. On the homeward journey he resolved to create a local crematorium. This he achieved, creating a facility which matched that of established funeral directors even with a book of remembrance. He had a very individualistic approach to returning of the ashes. He took considerable care to enquire from pet owners if their preference was for a simple but strong paper bag, a velvet pouch or a hand-made casket to which an optional extra was the provision of a felt mat so that the casket could be safely rested on a mantlepiece. Following the loss of our pet, the casket was delivered with a flower on top. My wife was very touched.

One lady was far from touched when her departed pet was returned to her, as was our practice, in a strong black bag ensuring it would not fall out. She made it very clear that returning her much loved family pet in a 'bin bag' was heartless beyond belief. She was never seen again.

A local vet has adapted part of his practice premises as a quiet room well away from the reception area, where clients can say goodbye to their pets in a private non-clinical setting. The room is filled with soft furnishings and a Memory Book for those who wish to remember their pets in such a manner. Owners are able to stay with their pets for as long or as little time as they wish prior to leaving via a door leading directly to the car park. Frequently it was the very emotionally distressed owners, following the loss of their pets, who vowed that they would never have another pet. Many did, often very quickly. They had suffered sorrow and sadness, but with the passage of time they found solace in a new pet.

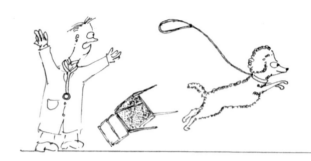

THE GREAT ESCAPE

As well as dealing with health issues, veterinary practices frequently provide a grooming service for both dogs and cats. A well-groomed pet radiates health, as well as being an indication of a caring owner. Our practice was no exception, with two experienced groomers, both of whom provided an excellent service.

One Wednesday during the mid-60s, a small white poodle from Sandilands Drive, a lower social area, arrived shortly after two p.m. Health and safety was not such a consideration at that time, so the dog's lead was tied to the leg of the receptionist's chair. However, the connection was insecure and when the office door was opened by a client, the dog made a lunge for freedom and was off, lead and all, to investigate Kittybrewster. Although I was not responsible for the dog's escape, the boss made it very clear that it was the remit of the youngest vet to find the animal!

In those days, Kittybrewster was an active part of Aberdeen. As well as the veterinary surgery, there was the Mart, the Astoria Picture House, the Northern Hotel, and a number of family concerns, including McDonald's the fruit shop, Kemp the plumber, Shirrifs the builder, Michie the chemist, Lyon the blacksmith, as well as a pub, railway station and post office.

My frantic search around the shops proved fruitless, but a porter at the station gave me some hope, as he had seen a white dog on the main railway line to Inverness. Walking along the railway line, it was not too long before I found the dog, just before the bridge at St Machar Drive.

I was delighted, but my delight turned to complete horror when I discovered the dog had only three legs. A railway engine had performed a neat, precise, amputation!

Returning to the surgery, I learned that the owner was coming to collect the dog at five p.m. This created a problem, as that was the time I had arranged to meet my long-suffering girlfriend, to visit Henderson the jeweller to look at an engagement ring. But romance had to give way to the stark realities of explaining to the owner how her dog, instead of being trimmed, was not only untrimmed, but also devoid of a front leg (not an eventuality covered in the veterinary course).

I am not quite sure whether it was easier to console the owner or to pacify my girlfriend. Somehow, the owner was reassured that her dog would adapt to almost its previous mobility and, in the fullness of time would have its trim without cost being a concern. An offer she accepted.

It was slightly more difficult for my girlfriend to reassure her mother that I would turn up for our appointment. When we finally arrived at Union Street, the day was further complicated by our lack of foresight that, it being a Wednesday, Hendersons was shut for a half day! The ring was selected the following day. Personally, I could not understand all the fuss the day before — it was the same week, after all.

The saga of the three-legged dog continued. After a meal at a veterinary function we were approached by the wife of the Peterhead vet. She was somewhat eager to inform us that among the dogs trimmed in their practice was the only three-legged dog in the area. They of course took great care of their dogs, unlike a known practice in Aberdeen. It was uplifting, however, to learn the owner of the three-legged dog was very appreciative of the care, attention and consideration of the young Aberdeen vet.

Almost fifty years later some of those involved are no longer with us. Happily, my girlfriend is now my wife and the ring is as bright as ever.

A DOGGIE NIGHTMARE

It was eleven pm when the telephone rang. A highly agitated caller pleaded with me, "Come, because my dog has been attacked by another dog."

Aware that the caller's dog was a bull terrier, my first thought was that it must have been some fight.

Before I could get out the door, the telephone rang again, the request being concise and abrupt, "Need you now. My dog has been injured in a fight and is bleeding badly."

As I did not know the caller I enquired as to the

contact details and the type of dog — Alsatian was the reply.

The two apparently sleeping policemen appeared to wake up when I passed their stationary car. On arrival at the surgery I thought I might well require their assistance.

While the dogs were subdued, their owners were not, being engaged in a vicious verbal battle with many words I was not even aware existed. Maybe that was why the policemen disappeared.

It was a case of first come first served so I started with the bull terrier. It was not too badly injured with no wounds requiring to be stitched and initial treatment to be followed by a check-up in forty-eight hours. The more difficult problem was the owner. He was a regular client who took great pleasure in informing all that he was an oil executive with a very good job, this being reflected by the fact he always paid by cheque.

At that point, however he was incandescent with rage departing with the audible warning that he "would see his solicitor in the morning".

The Alsatian had been more seriously injured, with immediate surgery being required. Although I had not met the owner his accent indicated he was from the Glasgow area.

It was not long before he informed me that, after retiring from full-time professional football, he had bought a guest house which was used by a steady stream of roustabouts on their way to the oil rigs. Although he encountered all types of people from across the world the presence of the dog prevented any problems. He indicated that as his guests paid cash, so would he. With the start of the oil boom such roustabouts were highly paid with one client ecstatic that he could "now buy his wife a fur coat".

In the following month the bull terrier failed to respond to treatment, eventually developing diabetes as a result of a prolonged shock effect and finally, with the consent of the family, quietly and peacefully made its way to the eternal kennel in the sky.

By that time, the angry owner had enlisted the assistance of his solicitor, from whom there was a steady stream of letters which the guest house owner later admitted to having "just put in the bin".

Shortly after, the oil executive's world collapsed when at short notice he was instructed to "clear his desk". With loss of the very good job with the consequential absence of income, there was an end to his expensive life style and no cheque book.

When I last saw him, he was working as a doorman at a local supermarket and appeared somewhat shamefaced to be seen.

The Alsatian, despite its severe injuries, made good progress and within four weeks was back to normal. There was a slight problem — no cash payment. In such cases, one had to pluck up enough courage to visit the address to remind the client that payment was due. (Nowadays debt collection agencies are utilised.)

True to his word the owner paid cash but only after he had removed it from the pay phone on the wall. Quite how he matched up the meter reading with the reduced amount of cash was his problem and not mine. Surprisingly, this was quite a legitimate practice.

With the decline of the oil boom the owner of the guest house decided to return to the west of Scotland but, prior to leaving, called in to say, "Thank you for attending to my dog that night." He told me he intended to open a corner shop — only cash, no credit and no cheques.

Generally, the fact you could match up the owners with their pets still seems to hold true but it was advisable to realise that, in Aberdeen, those who appeared to have most had least while those who had most, lived as if they had least.

PETS AT THE PALACE

The majority of owners look after their pets as part of the family, which in turn promotes the health benefits of exercise for the family. Unfortunately, some animals do not have the care and attention they require, which is when the Animal Welfare Agencies provide guidance and education.

Although the first Animal Welfare Bill was proposed in 1809, it was almost thirty years later before the Scottish Society for the Prevention of Cruelty to Animals was founded (SSPCA). The Aberdeen Association was formed in 1870 (AAPCA). The addition of Mrs. Murray's Home for Stray Dogs and Cats (now Mrs. Murray's Cat and Dog Home) in 1889 assisted greatly as a place of refuge and shelter for lost and stray dogs in the city and county of Aberdeen.

The founder of the home was a Mrs. Susan Murray, the widow of an Aberdeen advocate, Andrew Murray. The initial refuge was in the grounds of the family home of Inverdon House at Bridge of Don.

The increasing requirement led to the creation of new Kennels at 616 King Street opened by the Lord Provost in September of 1889.

Following the death of Mrs. Murray in 1919, her step-daughter, Miss Elizabeth Murray, became responsible for the running of the home. Due to her failing health a management committee was formed in 1926. The development of a council estate on the site of the home in the mid-1930s, resulted in a final move to Brickfield, East Seaton. It was officially opened by the Lady Provost in 1935.

On the death of Elizabeth Murray in 1936, the management committee supervised the operation of the home, an arrangement which continues to this day.

It was considered a privilege to be a committee member and was anathema to consider a fee. There has been continuity via various legal firms in the city of company secretaries and treasurers. The longest serving secretary/treasurer was the ebullient Robert Cattenach from 1956 until 1993.

For forty years Armstrong and Gammack the veterinary surgeons provided their services.

Neither Mrs. Murray's Cat and Dog Home nor the SSPCA receive government or Lottery funding. They are both self-funded with support from the public, commercial concerns as well as professional firms.

A novel idea to raise funds for the Cat and Dog Home and the Aberdeen Association for the Prevention of Cruely to Animals (AAPCA) originated from the manager of the Palace Cinema.

He suggested taking dogs from the home to the cinema to encourage punters to make a contribution to both organisations.

The home selected the dogs, which included a yappie Yorkshire terrior, a sullen spaniel and an aristocratic Airedale, however, transport of this varied cargo provided a challenge for the AAPCA.

The home has one unique item on its calendar. The support of some thirty local firms such as Northsound Radio, Aberdeen Spiritualist Centre, and the general public to an annual Christmas Food Appeal, which enables the 'residents' to enjoy a special meal of chicken, turkey, mini-sausages and even salmon.

When the AAPCA merged with the SSPCA a suggestion was made that Mrs. Murray's Cat and Dog Home should be included so as to create a single organisation within the Aberdeen area. This suggestion was refused by the management committee and the then secretary Ronald Cattanach, making it abundantly clear to the slick Edinburgh directors that no deal was "on the table" then or in the future.

And so Mrs. Murray's Cat and Dog Home ploughs its own furrow, although it is interesting that John Carle the Chief Inspector of the Scottish Society was initially an inspector with the Aberdeen Society and a son of the Carle family which managed the Cat and Dog Home for thirty years. Mrs. Susan Murray and her step- daughter Elizabeth would be proud.

WEIRD AND WONDERFUL

It is rumoured that a veterinary surgeon, on discussion with a client about his pet's ailment was so angered that the only treatment considered useful was the provision of Yellow Pages enabling another vet to be located — a no charge consultation.

While never having the courage to follow his example, life could have been so much easier if a section of the trusty Yellow Pages (unfortunately no longer published) listed a section on exotic pets. Inexperienced receptionists could be unnerved by young children requesting the vet to help with an iguana only later to discover that it was another name for a lizard. Such children were generally accompanied by a reluctant parent amazed that the cost of the consultation was greater than that of several pets.

Gerbils are difficult to handle — they can bite with amazing speed thereby inflicting considerable discomfort. It is documented that a vet, when bitten, threw the pet to the floor where it promptly expired. The owners subsequently made a complaint to the Royal College of Veterinary Surgeons resulting in the vet having to justify his action to the Disciplinary Committee. They concluded that it was a natural reflex reaction and dismissed the complaint.

However, a more embarrassing incident was the issue levelled against myself. It was more the comment from the local primary school, "Some vet your dad is. He doesn't know the difference between a rabbit and a guinea pig," which wounded the most. Initially our children had one guinea pig each, but disaster struck when the male guinea pig died suddenly. By chance, the following day a young rabbit was taken to the surgery having been found in a local garden. This was truly a gift from above as it could join the sole guinea pig. All was well until two weeks later when several young appeared one morning. I was of the opinion that they were guinea pigs as the rabbit was too young to be pregnant. Our son arrived at school with the news, arranging with his pals to sell the guinea pigs when they were ready. A problem arose when the "guinea pigs" developed long ears and could only be rabbits.

Why anyone should have a rat for a pet was beyond my comprehension: however, there were several clients who did. Such was the importance of one pet rat in a household that when it became unwell out of hours the owner summoned a taxi to take the rat to the vet's house for treatment. Fortunately, it survived, but I often wondered who was more surprised — the vet or the taxi driver.

Two animals I was very apprehensive about visiting were snakes and monkeys. The snakes, provided the owner restrained them, responded well to a vitamin injection, so that was a relief. Monkeys were not so easy to treat. Above all else my approach was to avoid handling them as they were very agile with the ability to inflict sudden painful bites. Thank goodness for the availability of oral drugs, which could be added to the drinking water.

Our neighbour relates an incident from his time in Kenya where it was quite common for colonial farmers to have pet monkeys, which could be a great source of entertainment. One evening his hostess was a very pompous, wealthy lady who liked to dominate the evening's conversation. She was unaware that, as the evening progressed, the pet monkey on her shoulder slowly and carefully unravelled a loose thread on her jumper. The guests had great difficulty in restraining their mirth when, on rising from the table, the sleeve of the jumper fell off.

It is generally believed that pets are a mirror image of their owners. What conclusion therefore can be formed about those who have exotic pets?

WOMEN, WHISKY AND WEDDINGS

It was a Thursday evening when I was summoned to visit a pup in a suburb of Aberdeen. Within a well-furnished front room, I discovered that the pup was a present for the fiancée of the well-dressed man who had requested the visit. He informed me that the pup had been purchased from a very reputable dog breeder in the south of Scotland and he had driven it to Aberdeen as quickly as possible, interrupting his journey only to buy not only a dog's bed, but some toys, as well as several tins of Pal dog food.

He was unaware that Pal had been formulated to "Prolong Active Life" of adult dogs and not pups. If fed to pups it would very quickly cause severe diarrhoea. The pup was subdued, had a slight tremor, increased respiratory rate but no overt indication of infection. General advice was given with regard to feeding as well as overall care with the suggestion that the situation should be reviewed in forty-eight hours. The rather forceful gentleman informed me that this would not be possible as that was the day of his wedding, the pup being a surprise present for his wife who he described as "dog daft". He intended to take the pup to both the ceremony and the reception but agreed to make contact if a problem arose. A not unexpected problem did arise when the pup developed sickness and diarrhoea in their bed during the night.

He was more than a little upset when he called the following morning to claim that the pup (and the vet) had ruined the start of his honeymoon and that his wife was most upset. Deciding to take matters into his own hands, he had arranged with a friend to take the pup for the next two weeks so that he and his wife would be able to enjoy their honeymoon without anxiety. If a problem arose, he should take the pup to another vet — one who was able to treat the pup successfully. Perhaps I was not cut out to be a marriage counsellor.

Stag parties were unpredictable. For reasons best known to a class mate and his fiancée they elected to combine the stag party with the hen party — a potentially unwise, if not dangerous idea. This took the form of an evening cruise on the Maid of the Loch on Loch Lomond (very tame by today's standards) with the unique scenery enhanced by music and refreshments. Those passengers who were accompanied by their wives were unimpressed by the ability of several young vets to consume considerable amounts of alcohol — to not only be able to stand but also to "chat up" several young ladies in their company. This did not accord with the professional persona of their esteemed veterinary surgeon (had they but known). The evening, however, was somewhat marred by the potential groom's attentiveness to the bridesmaid — a pre-marital divorce almost ensued.

In practice, regular off-time and invitations to weddings were difficult to arrange. Frequently this required the employment of a locum — "creatures" who varied from good, bad to the totally hopeless. One of the latter, a lady devoted to animals, endeared herself to my girlfriend when shortly before departure to a wedding, she telephoned requesting assistance with a caesarian section. This procedure was well within her capability but she was terrified of making an error having been totally unnerved by my reaction when she had telephoned early that morning to ask for help. She had not only locked herself out of the car but also the flat. The caesarian was completed successfully and my girlfriend, now wife, learned the pleasures of practice. The locum was not re-employed.

The combination of a wedding in Orkney followed by another in Glasgow two days later did pose certain logistical problems. The mixture of an evening wedding at 7.00 p.m., vast volumes of Highland Park whisky and a nightmare crossing in the Pentland Firth resulted in several difficulties. On leaving the ferry, the buildings were most certainly moving up and down, with Glasgow a long way away. Black coffee assisted matters but we only got as far as Dingwall before fatigue overcame us. Fortunately, we located an old-fashioned house with an equally old-fashioned lady who was more concerned about her sick cat than overnight visitors. Announcing in public that you are a vet can be problematic, but on this occasion it was a godsend, both to the lady and to ourselves, as reassurance about her cat not only made the two rooms available (no share without wedding ring) but also a meal. An early start assisted the onward journey, at least until we reached Luss, where we were delayed by a CND protest.

A slightly greater difficulty arose when dressing for the wedding in the Moss Bros outfit — the trousers were too large and no braces were included. A request for a piece of string was overheard by the house owner who noticed her next-door neighbour cutting his grass and wearing braces — her appeal for assistance resulted in the string being exchanged for braces with the neighbour wearing the string. We reached the wedding in time, the most memorable feature of the event being that the groom was so totally overcome by the emotion of the day that he was unable to deliver his speech. His wife took over, as she still does today.

We recently received a "Save the Date" invitation (quite unknown in our day). It was an indication we should reserve the date for an invitation to a wedding in Ireland the following year. We intend to do so. I do hope no leprechauns appear requiring treatment.

IT SHOULDN'T HAPPEN TO A VET'S VOLVO

It had been a bad day, nothing went right. Looked at something. It went wrong. Touched something, it went wrong. The final straw was a late urgent summons to Netherley to attend to a very sick cow. It had been ill for four days.

Into the trusty Volvo and off to Netherley via the Stonehaven Road. Unfortunately, at the Bridge of Dee a policeman who was perhaps having a quiet night, was concerned at the speed of the Volvo and he contacted the traffic section for assistance. The result being that two cars arrived at the farm, one with flashing blue lights. Well, the farmer did say hurry, so maybe he thought the police were assisting when they drew up behind my car.

The police car was straight out of *Z Cars*, a top of the range Ford Zephyr Zodiac. The officers, having been informed of the urgent nature of the visit, were of the opinion that it was most important that I should accompany them to their car. Difficult to refuse as there were two of them and they seemed to be very tall.

The officer asked my address, age and name. Due to the fact that I have five names, that page in his black notebook filled up quickly. The next page did not as it had only to record a negative breath test result. The officer indicated that speeding offences were taken rather seriously in the Stonehaven area, so a report would be sent to the Procurator Fiscal the next day. He then indicated to his colleague that he should open the rear door. Before he did so, I suggested to the officers that it was reasonable for me to record their names and numbers. Such information could be noted in my diary which was produced with a certain flourish. This would enable me to lodge a complaint with their senior officer to the effect that the action of his officers had delayed urgent treatment to an animal under my care. Numbers were given but no names. Don't have any? By now they could not get rid of this vet quickly enough.

As my car was obstructing the exit, it was necessary to adjust the position of their car. Having lost his composure, the driver engaged reverse gear, but omitted to follow the basic sequence of mirror, signal, manoeuvre, thus reversing somewhat speedily into the farmyard midden. The sight of a large police car stuck fast at an angle of forty-five degrees in a midden was unbelievable. Even more so was the sight of two very irate police officers up to their knees in manure as they made their way out of the midden. They declined my offer of help.

At last I was able to attend to the cow which really did require attention and subsequently recovered. Then time to return home, unlike the police officers, whose return to their station was only made possible by the arrival at 2 a.m. of a crane from Stonehaven.

I then had a suspicion that I was likely to be "a marked man" in possession of "a marked car". It was time for a change of car. At that time the Volvo dealer was David Gillanders in Fraser Place. He had the ability to sell sand to those who lived in the desert. It was not difficult therefore to agree a trade-in price for a new Volvo. The day the new car had to be collected was busy and unfortunately outside Peterculter, the sturdy Volvo suffered a major mechanical malfunction, or as a colleague said later, "the engine blew up". Consequently, the trade-in car arrived in Fraser Place on a car transporter. Mr Gillanders was totally unfazed and merely pointed to the new car.

Shortly after I was summoned to appear at Stonehaven Court.

In Aberdeen, assistance can come from the most unexpected quarter. I mentioned the issue to Mr Gillanders who on learning that speeds of 100mph were claimed by the police officers declared, "It was not possible". With the gearing in that type of Volvo the maximum speed it could achieve was 85 mph. He then said he knew a good lawyer. With the technical information from the car dealer, the lawyer persuaded the sheriff I was only doing my job, while the traffic officers were possibly somewhat overzealous — look where it landed them.